莉瑪的辣椒

LIMA'S RED HOT CHILLI

written by David Mills

Chinese translation by Sylvia Denham

mantra

莉瑪放學回家時覺得肚子餓。
「我肚子餓呀！」她說。

When Lima got home from school
she felt hungry.
"I feel hungry!" she said.

「廚房裏有很多食物呀！」媽媽叫道。
「但不要吃紅辣椒啊！」

"Plenty of food in the kitchen!" shouted her mother.
"But don't eat the red hot chilli!"

莉瑪於是走入廚房找東西吃。

她看到一個未剝殼的椰子，
但它實在⋯太硬了。

So Lima went to the kitchen for a nibble.

She found a hairy brown coconut
But it was just ... too hard.

油光滑膩的咖厘角
實在⋯太凍了。

The shiny samosas
Were just ... too cold.

吃那罐意大利粉
又實在…太麻煩。

The can of spaghetti
Was just … too difficult.

而那些粘膩的糖果
實在放得太高了。

And the sticky sweets
Were just ... too high up for Lima.

跟著她看到了，
那個最美妙、光亮、鮮紅的東西！
那紅辣椒。

Then she saw it.
The most delicious, shiny, red ... thing!
The RED HOT CHILLI.

靜悄悄地，偷偷地，
莉瑪把它放入口裏。

Quietly and secretly
Lima popped it into her mouth.

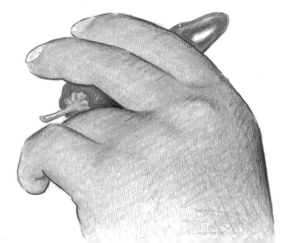

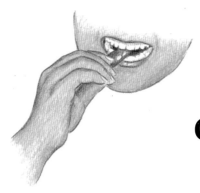

嘎扎！

Crunch!

但她不能再偷偷摸摸了。

But she could not keep her secret very long!

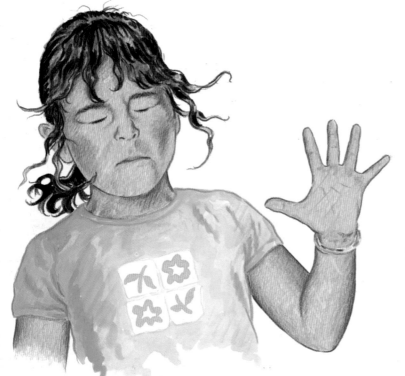

莉瑪的臉越來越熱，

Lima's face got hotter and hotter and hotter and...

嘴巴霧出火花。

...fireworks flew out of her mouth!

她的媽媽走來幫她，
「水，水，試試喝一些水。」

Her Mother came to help.
"Water, water, try some water!"

於是莉瑪吞下一整杯冰凍的水，
這實在好極了…
但她的嘴巴仍然很燙！

So Lima swallowed a whole glass of cold cold water
Which was nice ...
But her mouth was still too hot!

她的爸爸跟著也來幫她，
「雪糕，雪糕，試試吃一些雪糕。」

Then her Dad came to help.
"Ice cream, ice cream, try some ice cream!"

於是莉瑪吃了很多冰凍的雪糕，
這實在好極了⋯
但她的嘴巴仍然很燙！

So Lima ate dollops of freezing ice cream
Which was lovely ...
But her mouth was still too hot!

跟著姨媽也來幫她，
「遮厘，遮厘，試試遮厘！」

Then her Aunty came to help.
"Jelly, jelly, try some jelly!"

於是莉瑪吃了一大堆冰凍遮厘。
這實在美味⋯
但她的嘴巴依然很燙！

So Lima ate mountains of wobbly jelly
Which was yummy ...
But her mouth was still too hot!

跟著祖父也來幫她，
「芒果，芒果，試試吃一些芒果！」

Then her Grandad came to help.
"Mango, mango, try some mango!"

於是莉瑪吃下一整個多汁的芒果，
這實在甜美 ...
但她的嘴巴還是很燙！

So Lima ate a whole juicy mango
Which was delicious ...
But her mouth was still too hot!

最後她的祖母也來幫她，
「牛奶，牛奶，試試牛奶！」

At last her Grandma came to help.
"Milk, milk, try some milk!"

於是莉瑪飲了一大壺凍奶，
跟著…慢慢地

So Lima drank a huge jug of cool milk.
Then slowly ...

莉瑪露出一個香甜的笑容，
「呀！」莉瑪說，「沒有紅辣椒了。」
「啐！」各人鬆一口氣。

Lima smiled a milky smile.
"Ahhhh!" said Lima. "No more red hot chilli."
"Phew!" said everyone.

「你是否仍然肚子餓呢？」莉瑪的媽媽問道。
「不餓了，」莉瑪捧著肚子答道，「只是有點飽呢！」

"Now," said Lima's Mum, "are you still hungry?"
"No," said Lima, holding her belly. "Just a bit full!"

For Lima, who inspired the story
D.M.
To all the Brazells and Mireskandaris,
especially Shadi, Babak & Jaleh, with love
D.B.

First published by Mantra Publishing 1999
This edition published 2003
All rights reserved
Printed in Italy

Mantra Publishing
5 Alexandra Grove
London N12 8NU
http:www.mantrapublishing.com